WALT DISNEY'S
ALICE in WONDERLAND

Adapted by Teddy Slater

Illustrated by Franc Mateu

A GOLDEN BOOK • NEW YORK

Western Publishing Company, Inc., Racine, Wisconsin 53404

One golden spring day a young girl named Alice
was sitting by the river, listening to her sister
read aloud from a history book. At least, that's
what Alice was supposed to be doing. Instead,
she was playing with Dinah, her cat, which was
more fun.

"I wish you could talk back to me, Dinah,"
she said. "I'm sure you would have many
interesting things to say."

The sun was so bright, and the air was so
warm, that Alice was soon daydreaming. Slowly
her head began to nod.

She snapped to attention, however, when a large white rabbit went dashing by. Strangely, he was wearing a waistcoat and a bow tie and carrying a huge pocket watch. Even more strangely, he was talking to himself!

"I'm late, I'm late, for a very important date," the White Rabbit muttered as he went along.

In a flash, Alice was on her feet, chasing after him.

Still fretting, the rabbit took a giant hop into a
hollow tree, exclaiming, "Oh, my fur and
whiskers! I'm late, I'm late, I'm late!"

Alice thought that he might be late for a party,
so she followed him into the tree.

Suddenly Alice stumbled, then tumbled head over heels into a deep hole. After a while, instead of falling faster, she began to fall slower and slower—until she was floating more than falling.

Alice landed gently, just in time to see the rabbit's white puff of a tail disappear behind a tiny door.

Since she was too big to follow the White Rabbit, Alice wandered off by herself.

Alice soon discovered that she had entered a strange and wondrous land. It was full of the oddest creatures she had ever seen. There were talking birds and walking fish. There was also a Cheshire cat, with the widest of grins, who kept appearing and disappearing. And sometimes only the cat's grin could be seen.

Alice thought the creatures all seemed quite at home in this topsy-turvy Wonderland. She hoped one of them could help her find the White Rabbit, but they were no help at all.

Alice walked through a forest and came across
a pair of roly-poly twins. Their names were
written on their collars. "I see that you are
Tweedledee and Tweedledum," she greeted them.

"When first meeting someone, you should
shake hands and state your name and business,"
said Tweedledum, grabbing Alice's hand.

"That's manners!" said Tweedledee, grabbing
her other hand.

With that, the tubby twins danced Alice
around and swept her off her feet. But they were
so rough that they flipped her over and knocked
her onto her back. Alice was not amused.

"Talk about manners!" Alice exclaimed as she picked herself up and brushed herself off. "If you must know, my name is Alice, and I'm following the White Rabbit. I'm very sorry, but I must go."

Despite the twins' protests, Alice went on her way. Soon she came to an unusual garden. Flitting about were bread-and-butterflies and a rocking-horse fly. Then Alice discovered that the flowers of Wonderland could speak!

"What kind of flower are you?" a big red rose asked her.

"Oh, I'm not any kind of flower," Alice replied.

"No fragrance," a daisy said, sniffing at Alice's hair.

"But I'm not a flower," Alice repeated.

"Just as I suspected!" the rose cried. "She's nothing but a common weed!"

"Leave!" shouted all the flowers together. "We don't want you in our lovely garden."

Alice was forced to run away.

Near the garden Alice saw a familiar grin up in a tree. It was the Cheshire Cat. When the rest of him appeared, Alice said, "Have you seen the White Rabbit?"

"No," said the Cheshire Cat. "But if I were looking for him, I'd ask the Mad Hatter."

"I'm not sure I want to visit a mad person," said Alice.

"You can't avoid it," said the cat. "Mostly everyone here is mad." And with that, the cat began to disappear.

When the cat had completely disappeared, Alice realized that he hadn't told her how to find the Mad Hatter.

As she wandered on she saw two road signs pointing in the same direction. One read "Mad Hatter" and the other read "March Hare." Alice still had no wish to meet a Mad Hatter, but she hoped the March Hare might know the mysterious White Rabbit, too.

Alice followed the signs to a clearing in the woods where the Mad Hatter was giving a tea party.

"No room!" the Mad Hatter howled as Alice plopped down in one of the many chairs around the table.

"But there's plenty of room," Alice protested.

"Perhaps," the March Hare admitted. "But it's very rude to sit down without first being invited."

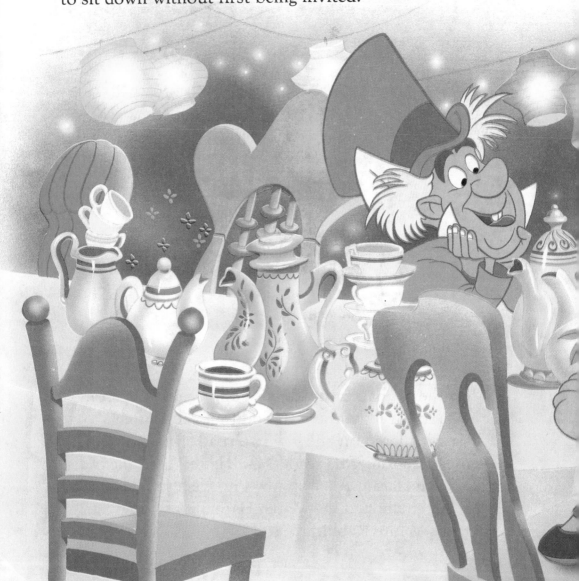

The Hatter and the Hare then proceeded to make Alice feel quite unwelcome. They not only refused to give her any tea, but it was clear that they had no intention of helping her find the White Rabbit. So once again, Alice set off on her own.

Alice soon came across one of the strangest creatures she'd meet in this very strange land—the Queen of Hearts. Though the queen was dressed like an ordinary queen in an ordinary deck of cards, she was most regal as she ordered her subjects around.

The queen was playing an odd game of croquet. The wickets were cards, the balls were hedgehogs, and the mallets were flamingos.

When the queen invited Alice to play, she thought it might be fun, but it wasn't! Alice's flamingo refused to cooperate, and the queen turned out to be a terrible sport. "Off with his head!" she cried the minute anyone displeased her.

Alice considered leaving the game, since she very much wanted to keep her head. But she also wanted to meet the White Rabbit, who she felt was very near indeed.

As it turned out, Alice did see the White Rabbit. He was working for the queen. Alice was just about to introduce herself to him when the Cheshire Cat made another of his unannounced appearances.

Alice watched in horror as the mischievous cat tripped up the queen and then promptly disappeared. And when the queen turned accusing eyes on Alice, crying, "Off with her head!" Alice decided it was time for her, too, to disappear.

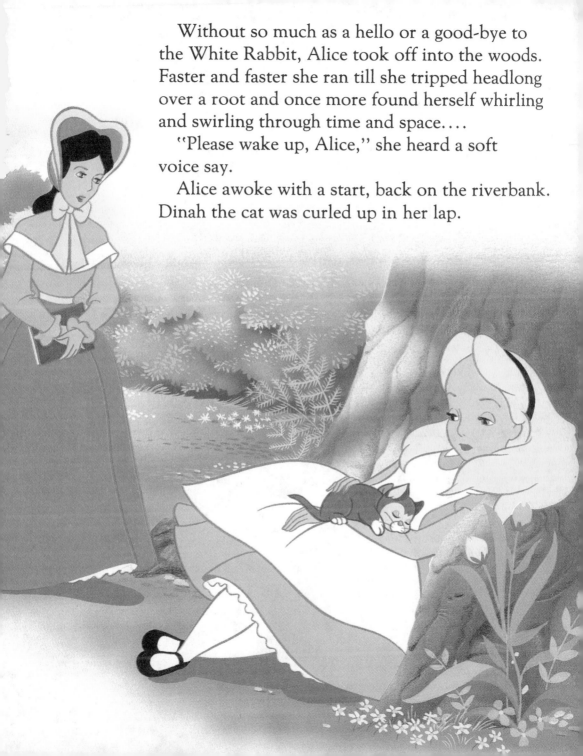

Without so much as a hello or a good-bye to the White Rabbit, Alice took off into the woods. Faster and faster she ran till she tripped headlong over a root and once more found herself whirling and swirling through time and space....

"Please wake up, Alice," she heard a soft voice say.

Alice awoke with a start, back on the riverbank. Dinah the cat was curled up in her lap.

"You've been dreaming," said Alice's sister.

"Oh, dear," Alice cried. "I must have fallen asleep while you were reading to me."

"It's been a long day," said her sister. "No wonder you're tired. Why don't we just go home now and have our tea?"

"I seem to have lost my taste for tea," Alice said, recalling the Mad Hatter's tea party, "but I certainly would like to go home."

Alice's sister gave her a puzzled look. Then she took Alice's hand, and they walked home together.